This book belongs to

_____

_____

This edition published by Parragon Books Ltd in 2015

Parragon Books Ltd
Chartist House
15–17 Trim Street
Bath BA1 1HA, UK
www.parragon.com

ISBN 978-1-4723-8201-6

Printed in China

Disney · PIXAR MOVIE COLLECTION
A SPECIAL DISNEY STORYBOOK SERIES

Cars 2

PaRragon

Bath · New York · Cologne · Melbourne · Delhi
Hong Kong · Shenzhen · Singapore · Amsterdam

British secret agent Finn McMissile had received a distress call from a fellow agent. Finn travelled to the agent's location in the middle of the Pacific Ocean. He was stowed away on an attack ship that was heading towards an oil rig.

Using his grappling hooks and magnetic wheel armour, Finn silently drove up the side of the rig. As he reached the upper levels, he realized there were hundreds of oil rigs surrounding him!

Finn hid inside the rig and observed a wanted criminal called Professor Z. Lying beside the Professor and his crew was a special TV camera. Then Finn saw a fellow agent – he had been crushed into a cube of scrap metal!

Suddenly, Professor Z spotted Finn and sent his gang after him. When they cornered Finn, he leaped off the rig, turned into a submarine and escaped!

Meanwhile, in the town of Radiator Springs, Mater had called
all of his friends together to welcome home his very best friend,
Lightning McQueen.

Lightning was a famous racing car and he had just won the Hudson
Hornet Memorial Piston Cup! Mater couldn't wait to see him.

When Lightning arrived, everyone went to the Wheel Well restaurant, where they watched a TV show. Mater called in to the show to defend his best friend against Francesco Bernoulli, an Italian racing car who swore he was faster than Lightning.

Soon, Lightning had agreed to race against Francesco in a three-event race hosted by former oil tycoon, Sir Miles Axlerod – the World Grand Prix.

Mater, Luigi, Guido, Fillmore and Sarge quickly offered to be Lightning's pit crew. Soon "Team Lightning McQueen" headed to the first World Grand Prix event in Japan!

Lightning and his friends had a fantastic time sightseeing in the city of Tokyo. There were skyscrapers, neon lights, Kabuki theatre and high-tech gadgets!

Then they all went to a fancy welcome party.

Finn McMissile and Holley Shiftwell, another British agent, were also there. They were looking for an American agent who had some top-secret information for them.

At the party, Lightning wanted to make a good impression in front of Miles Axlerod. But Mater embarrassed him by leaking a huge puddle of oil on the floor!

Lightning sent Mater to the toilets to get cleaned up.

Professor Z's goons, Grem and Acer, had cornered the American agent Rod "Torque" Redline in the toilets. When Mater came in, the agent secretly stuck the device he was supposed to give to the British spies on Mater instead.

Later, Professor Z questioned Torque and guessed that the American agent had passed the device to Mater.

The Professor sent Grem and Acer to track down the tow truck and get the device back.

allinol

On the day of the race, Finn and Holley watched all the cars fill up with a new alternative fuel called Allinol. Sir Miles Axlerod, the inventor of Allinol, was hosting the World Grand Prix to introduce the fuel to the public.

Grem and Acer aimed Professor Z's special TV camera at one of the racing cars. But the camera wasn't really a camera at all! It shot out a beam of radiation that made the Allinol in the car boil and then explode! Then they aimed at another car, and another....

When Acer tried to grab Mater, Holley spoke to him through his headset and guided him out of the pits, where he'd been with the rest of Lightning's pit crew. Mater happily followed Holley's instructions – he thought he was meeting her for a date!

Grem and Acer suddenly started to close in on Mater, but Finn jumped in. Mater thought the fight was the best karate demonstration he'd ever seen!

Back at the race, Lightning lost to Francesco Bernoulli.
Lightning was upset that Mater had given him such bad
racing tips.
Lightning didn't realize that he'd been listening to Mater
commenting on Finn's fight with Grem and Acer!

Reporters surrounded Sir Miles Axlerod and asked him if Allinol was to blame for the engine explosions during the race. Miles insisted that his fuel was completely safe.

Meanwhile, Mater had returned to the pit garage and was trying to explain to Lightning what had just happened.

But Lightning didn't believe him. He was angry with Mater for making him lose the race.

Mater felt terrible. He left a goodbye note for Lightning and went to the airport to fly home.

Finn McMissile, who was disguised as an airport security guard, was waiting for Mater at the airport. Finn still thought Mater was a secret agent.

Suddenly, Grem and Acer arrived again and tried to capture Mater. Holley saved both Mater and Finn from the attack by whisking them off on a spy plane called Siddeley.

Back at the hotel, Lightning read Mater's note.
Lightning hadn't wanted Mater to leave, but at least
now he wouldn't have to worry about Mater getting
into trouble.

In fact, Mater was helping Finn and Holley. Together they looked at a holographic photo that was on the device that Torque had stuck to Mater.

Mater said the photo was of a poorly made, fuel-guzzling engine with some expensive new parts. But he didn't know who the engine belonged to.

Finn, Holley and Mater flew to Paris. Finn was hoping a black-market parts dealer called Tomber could tell them who the mysterious engine in the photo belonged to.

Mater explained that the engine belonged to a Lemon – a car that didn't work properly. Gremlins, Pacers, Hugos and Trunkovs were all types of Lemons. Tomber said there was going to be a big meeting of Lemons in Porto Corsa, which was also the location of the next World Grand Prix race!

Lightning and his crew soon arrived in Italy for the race. Their first stop was Luigi and Guido's hometown. Everyone came out to greet them!

Meanwhile, Holley was disguising Mater as one of the Lemons' tow trucks so that he could sneak into the meeting. She gave Mater lots of cool spy gadgets, too!

The next day, before the race in Porto Corsa, Lightning
admitted to Francesco Bernoulli that he really missed Mater.

Little did Lightning know, Mater was actually nearby. With his disguise, Mater had made it into the Lemon meeting held at a casino. Holley and Finn were waiting outside, listening in on the action through Mater's headset.

Professor Z introduced the Lemons to the Big Boss, who appeared on a TV screen. But only his engine was visible – the same engine that was in Torque's photo!

The Big Boss said that once Allinol was proven to be dangerous, all cars would use petrol again. Then the Lemons, who controlled the oil reserves, would finally get the wealth, respect and power that they deserved!

As the Big Boss spoke, Grem and Acer aimed the fake TV camera at Carla Veloso, the racing car from Brazil.

Finn raced to the top of the tower to stop Grem and Acer. As he leaped into the air to get to the Lemons, a helicopter captured him with a giant magnet!

Finn was taken away and Grem and Acer continued to aim at even more cars. Their next target was Shu Todoroki, the racer from Japan.

Shu's engine exploded!

At the race track finish line, Lightning shot across for the win.

By now, everyone thought Allinol was to blame for the explosions and crashes. But Lightning insisted he would use Allinol in the final race.

The Big Boss heard Lightning's statement and gave the order to destroy him.

Mater tried to leave and warn his friend. He had to escape using his spy gear!

Mater finally arrived at Porto Corsa, but before Lightning could spot him the Lemons hauled Mater away.

Mater was tied up inside a big clock called Big Bentley, along with Finn and Holley. They were in London, England, the location of the final race!

Grem and Acer told Mater that they had planted a bomb inside Lightning's pit at the race.

After the pair left, Mater managed to escape and rushed to save his friend!

Finn and Holley struggled to get free, too. Suddenly, they realized that the Lemons had let Mater escape on purpose. The bomb was actually on Mater and he was heading straight to Lightning!

Holley quickly extended her wings and burst straight through the clock face.

When Mater arrived at the pits, Lightning was so
happy to see him that he hooked himself on to his buddy.
Just then, Finn radioed to say the bomb was on Mater!
Mater had to leave before Professor Z could detonate the
bomb, so he rocketed off....

Meanwhile, Professor Z spotted Holley from his viewing box and then fled. Now it was up to Grem and Acer to do away with Lightning so that the Lemons could finally rise to power!

Holley flew off to help Mater, while Finn went after the Professor.

Professor Z fled to the river, where he attempted to escape on a combat ship.
Finn lassoed the Professor with cables and captured him!

Grem and Acer were seconds away from crashing into Mater and Lightning.

Holley flew down, hit the pavement and slammed into Grem and Acer. The Lemons went flying into the air and were defeated!

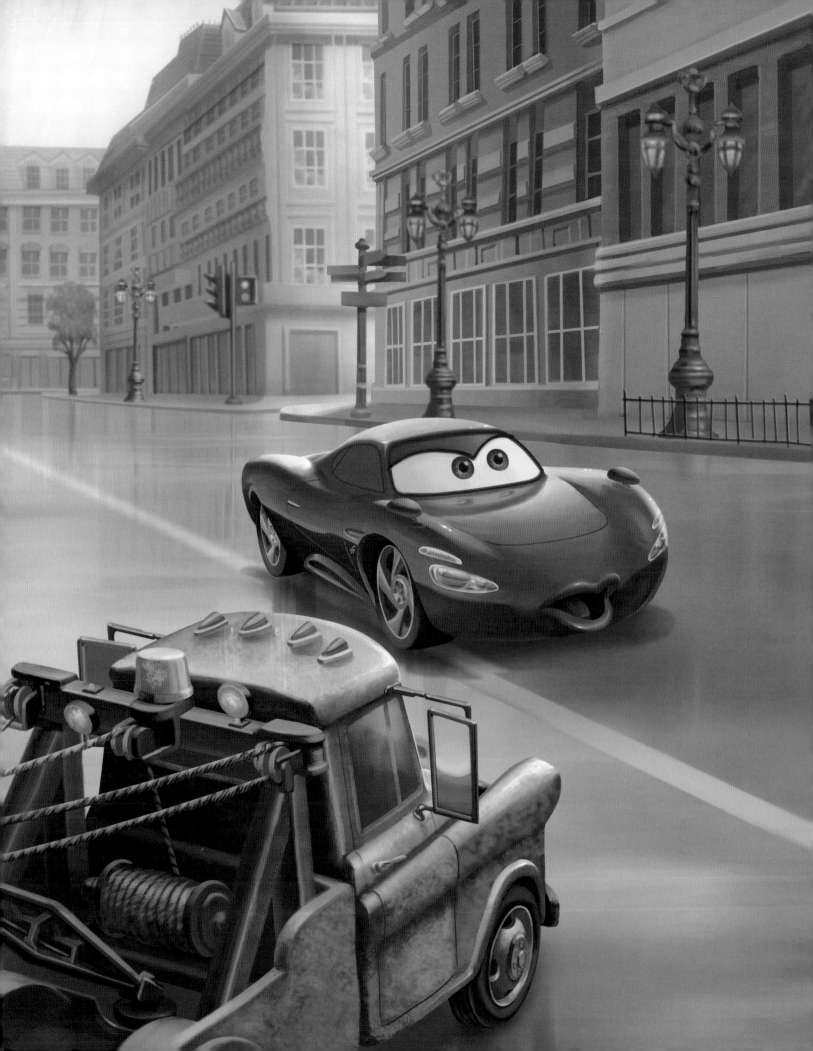

Finn arrived with Professor Z and ordered him to deactivate the bomb.

The Professor informed Finn that only the one who activated the bomb could turn it off – and that was *not* him.

Suddenly, Mater worked out who the Lemons' Big Boss was. He flew straight to Buckingham Palace with Lightning.

When Mater landed at the palace, Finn and the guards warned him to keep the bomb away from the queen.

Mater quickly explained that the engine in the photo belonged to Sir Miles Axlerod. Axlerod was the Big Boss and the biggest Lemon of all!

Mater went on to explain that Axlerod made Allinol look dangerous so that everyone would give up on alternative fuels and go back to using petrol – because then all the Lemons would get rich!

Axlerod was trapped and had no choice but to deactivate the bomb. Mater had saved the day! No one was prouder of him than Lightning. The queen thanked Mater by knighting him for his bravery!

Soon Mater, Lightning and the rest of their friends were back at home and preparing for the next big event: the Radiator Springs Grand Prix. Finn and Holley came to watch. They wanted Mater to join them on another spy mission, but the tow truck politely refused. He belonged in Radiator Springs with his best buddy, Lightning!